12/10

WITHDRAWN

Scraps of Time
1879

Away West

by

PATRICIA C. McKISSACK

illustrated by

GORDON C. JAMES

Viking

Viking

Published by Penguin Group

Penguin Young Readers Group, 345 Hudson Street,
New York, New York 10014, U.S.A.

Penguin Books Ltd, Registered Offices: 80 Strand, London WC2R 0RL, England

First published in 2006 by Viking, a division of Penguin Young Readers Group

1 3 5 7 9 10 8 6 4 2

LIBRARY OF CONGRESS CATALOGING-IN-PUBLICATION DATA
McKissack, Patricia C., date–
Away west / by Patricia C. McKissack; illustrated by Gordon C. James.
p. cm.—(Scraps of time)
Summary: In 1879, thirteen-year-old Everett Turner leaves a life of struggle on his
family's farm and runs away to St. Louis, where he works in a livery stable before
heading to the all-Black town of Nicodemus, Kansas.
ISBN 0-670-06012-7 (hardcover)
[1. Runaways—Fiction. 2. Brothers—Fiction. 3. Horses—Fiction. 4. African
Americans—Fiction. 5. West (U.S.)—History—1860–1890—Fiction.] I. Title. II. Series.
PZ7.M478693Awa 2006
[Fic]—dc22
2005023315

Printed in U.S.A.
Set in Excelsior
Book design by Nancy Brennan

To Francine Jordan and Steve Brodhage,
with thanks for all your help
—*P. C. McK.*

This book is for my younger sister Crystal, whom
I love. She has always been and continues to be
an inspiration to me.
—*G. C. J.*

Contents

In Gee's Attic

The Webster cousins loved Gee's big attic because there were so many old things in it. Their grandmother called them scraps of time.

Gee kept files of papers and photos, stacks of books, suitcases filled with old clothes, and boxes of toys and games—things that belonged to people in their family. Nearly all of them lived a long time ago. Many had died before Mattie Rae or her older cousins, Aggie and Trey, were born.

They were putting some of the scraps into a

scrapbook to take to the next Turner family reunion.

"The last time we were here," Trey said to Gee, "you promised to tell us about this." He had a box in his lap and was holding up an army medal.

"Whose was it?" Aggie asked.

"It belonged to my great-grandfather, Franklin Turner. He was a Civil War hero. He gave the medal to his son, my grandfather, Everett Turner. Everett's story begins in St. Louis, Missouri," said Gee. "He had just run away from home. It was January of eighteen seventy-nine. He was only thirteen, but he was determined to make it out West."

"Was he scared?" Mattie Rae looked worried. She hugged her stuffed rabbit, Alonzo.

"He should have been plenty scared, but he was too excited," said Gee.

Chapter 1

Stowaway

In the cold darkness, Everett sat squeezed between sacks of sugar, cotton, rice, and tea. All around him he heard mice squeaking and scurrying about. He forced himself not to move or cry out. That old saying about being as quiet as a mouse was dead wrong. He laughed to himself. Mice were really noisy.

Everett was a stowaway. He was hiding in the hold of a supply boat called the *Camel's Back*. It was headed up the Mississippi River to

St. Louis. He'd slipped onboard in Memphis the night before.

Everett's legs ached. He wanted to stand up and stretch, but he couldn't. He might be discovered. Then he'd be thrown overboard. Or worse, he might get sent back to Pearl, Tennessee. And no matter what, he wasn't going home. His future lay in the West.

That's what the handbill said. LAND. OPPORTUNITY. YOUR FUTURE IS IN THE WEST.

All Everett had was twenty-five cents and his pa's army medal. But he was heading west toward his future.

Everett knew he wouldn't have had the nerve to leave home if his brother Cole hadn't gone first. Cole had joined the army. His last letter said he was in Texas, heading for New Mexico. He was a sergeant in the Tenth Cavalry, and had a horse named Jimbo. The Tenth Cavalry was all-black, but all the officers were white. Their job was to keep peace in Indian territory. It was a dangerous job. Everett was proud of Cole.

It was January now. Everett would turn fourteen in July. So he felt older than just thirteen. Still, you had to be eighteen to enlist in the army. Four and a half years was a long time to wait. But he was determined to leave farming behind—*now*! He was sick of crop failures. Why couldn't his oldest brother, Gus, understand that?

"Pa left the farm to us," Gus had said the other night. "We don't have to sharecrop for nobody. We owe it to his memory to make the farm prosper."

Gus wasn't happy when Cole left. But Cole was a "man" and old enough to do as he wished.

So Everett was left stuck on the farm. And no matter how hard they worked the fields, the farm didn't prosper. The land seemed to be cottoned-out. Everett was tired of trying.

"I hate this place!" Everett yelled. "I'm leaving!"

Gus got angry. "Where to? You always jump into things without thinking and end up in trouble. One day I won't be around to help you. What then?"

Everett decided it was time to find out. The next day he ran away, made it to Memphis, and hid in the cargo hold of the *Camel's Back*.

Now, in a few hours, he would be in St. Louis, Missouri. And from there he'd be on his way out West.

He clasped the pouch in his pocket. In it was Pa's medal from fighting in the war. The Civil War.

"You're the only one of my boys born in free-dom. And you got the most schooling. It's why I fought in that terrible war. I want *you* to have this," Pa had said not long before he died.

Well, Pa always said being free meant leading the life you wanted. And that was just what Everett aimed to do.

Suddenly, a mouse scampered across his ankle. Its tiny little claws tickled his flesh. This made his leg jump, and he accidentally kicked over a barrel. The barrel knocked over another, and both hit the bottom of the hold with a crash.

"Somebody take a look down there," Everett heard a man say.

There was the sound of running footsteps. The hatch overhead opened. Blinding sunbeams burst through the darkness, shedding light on the cargo bay.

"Captain Brewer, sir!" the crewman shouted, looking down at Everett. "Look at the little mouse I found!"

nt

The next thing Everett knew he was being dragged before the captain—Captain Brewer, a white man with a belly as big as a barrel.

"Any papers on him?" the captain asked the crewman.

The crewman grabbed Everett and searched him. Then he threw him down on the deck, where Everett stayed kneeling. Everything in his pockets was handed over to the captain. But the only thing that interested the captain was Pa's medal.

"This is a Medal of Valor. Who'd you steal it from?"

"Nobody. It belonged to my pa," Everett said, raising his head just a little. He could tell the captain didn't believe him.

"What are you doing on my vessel?"

Now Everett kept his head bowed low. "I—I came onboard to see if I could find a job. Yes. That's it. But it was dark down there, and I just fell asleep."

"Don't you lie, boy," snapped the captain. He pulled Everett upright. "A lot of people died so you could be free. If this medal is yours, you should be ashamed of yourself."

"Should I pitch him overboard, sir?" the crewman asked.

"No, not yet," said Captain Brewer. Then,

turning to Everett, he said, "You can work off the passage, or the St. Louis police can decide what to do with you."

"I'll work," said Everett. He held out his hand for his medal.

But the captain said, "No. I'll be keeping this till you work off what you owe."

For the next week, Everett worked alongside the crew in the harbor of St. Louis. He helped unload sugar and coffee from the *Camel's Back*. Then the crew reloaded pork packed in lard, and corn and beans for the return trip to Memphis and on to New Orleans.

It was hard labor. Some days it snowed. Everett didn't own a coat. But one of the men found one for him in the trash. He was sore and cold and tired, but he didn't complain. He enjoyed hearing the men tell Mississippi River stories. And the crew liked to sing while they

worked. Old songs. Songs Everett knew from Gus and the elders back home.

In that great gittin' up morning,
Fare ye well, fare ye well.

There was no real church or preacher in Pearl. Most of the time folks just showed up at the Turners' farm on Sunday and listened to Gus lead a few prayers. People liked hearing Gus. His voice had power. His words were simple but full of faith.

Oh, in that great gittin' up morning,
Fare ye well, fare ye well.

Hearing the singing made Everett miss Gus. But not enough to go back home.

After a week, Everett's debt was paid. The

captain said, "I could use another strong hand. You're welcome to stay on . . . for pay, of course."

Everett thanked him but said no. Staying put wasn't going to get him West. "Sir, I'd like my medal back now."

The captain's eyes turned cold. "Where did your father fight?"

Everett could tell the captain still thought the medal was stolen. The man was testing him. "At Fort Negley in Nashville, Tennessee. My pa said colored soldiers stood firm and helped hold Nashville."

The captain grunted. "I know. I was there. Tell me now. Who was in command? General Hood, wasn't it?"

"Oh, no, sir," Everett replied right away. "General Hood fought for the South. Pa served under General Thomas."

Now the captain looked satisfied. He gave

the medal to Everett and flipped his quarter back to him as well. "How far do you think twenty-five cents will take you? And with pick-pockets all around town, I bet you won't even have that for long."

It didn't matter to Everett.

"Just remember," the captain said. "It's not your medal. You are only keeping it. You must earn the right to call it your own."

Everett put the medal in his front pocket where he always kept it. Whenever he was worried, he rubbed the medal. Like magic it made him feel better right away.

"Yes, sir," Everett said, although he wasn't sure what the captain meant. The medal *was* his. And he was doing what his pa would have wanted him to do. He was following his dream.

Chapter 3

—✦—

Rescued

St. Louis was a busy, churning city—the fourth largest in the country. It never seemed to slow down. People were always moving—walking, running, coming, going—always in a hurry.

Everett had been wandering around for almost an hour. His body ached from the cold, and he had no idea where to go. He needed to find other people who were heading West, too. For a moment, he thought maybe he should have signed on with the riverboat captain after all. But only for a moment.

He came to a street with buildings lined up like soldiers in a row. Some of them soared four and five stories high! Horses and carriages rattled along the cobblestone streets. Twice Everett had to leap out of the way of a speeding buggy.

Nothing, however, was more wonderful than the bridge. It went all the way across the Mississippi River. On the other side was Illinois. Everett had never seen anything like it.

But past the bridge, the neighborhood changed. The houses were rundown. There were no street signs. Two large men, one white and the other black, came stumbling out of a tavern. They were dressed like the men who worked on the riverboats. One of them looked up and spotted Everett.

Before he knew it, they were coming toward him, their fists raised.

"Look at what we gots here," said the white man. There was a tattoo of a wolf on his arm. "What're ye holding on to in yer pocket? Gold, is it?" He lunged toward Everett, but the boy jumped away. He squeezed the medal tightly and tried to run.

The black man had a scar running down his cheek like a bolt of lightning. He grabbed Everett's arms from behind. "I bet he's good for a dime or two."

The man with the tattoo found Everett's medal. "What this? Just junk from the War. Who cares!" He threw the medal on the ground. "But looky here—a whole quarter of a dollar. Where would a shrimp like you get that kind of money?"

Everett struggled.

"He probably stole it," said the other.

Everett squirmed and managed to kick the white man in the leg. The man cried out and drew back his fist.

"Give me back my money!" Everett hollered.

"Let that boy go," shouted someone nearby. "Link, you be on your way, 'fore you land in jail again. You, too, Murphy."

Everett felt the hold on his arms loosen. The men ran off, ducking between two buildings and mumbling under their breath.

The medal was lying in the dirt. Everett picked it up. "They stole my money," Everett told the young man. He was big and strong and looked to be Gus's age. Maybe eighteen or nineteen.

"Be glad they didn't steal your life," he said, and led Everett in the opposite direction. "I'm Billy Breeze."

Everett shook the hand offered to him. "Pleased to meet you, Billy Breeze. I'm Everett Turner. And I'm sure glad you showed up when you did. Thanks!"

"What are you doing in this part of town? You hoping to get West, aine you?"

"How'd you know?" Everett asked.

"All you Exodusters got the same hopeful look on your faces."

"What-a dusters?" Everett asked.

"Exoduster," Billy explained. "That's what they call black folks going off to Kansas. It's part *exodus*, which means leaving, and part *duster*, 'cause of the dusty trails you'll be traveling to get West."

Billy's friendly ways reminded Everett of Gus. But Billy laughed a little easier and didn't seem nearly so serious. He made Everett feel comfortable.

"I guess I am an Exoduster. If I had my way, I'd go now. Right this minute."

"Have you joined up with a group?" Billy asked.

"No . . . but I will. . . ."

"Talked to a trail leader?" Billy asked.

"Um, no. . . ."

"Did those thieves get all your money?" Now Billy was beginning to sound like Gus. Billy's brow was even creased just like Gus's.

Everett shook his head yes.

Billy threw up his hands. "That's the problem with you Exodusters," he said. "You come to St. Louis with no money, no food, and no plan. Just blind hope." Suddenly Billy stopped talking and walked away. Then he came back. "Where're you staying?"

"I'll find someplace," Everett said, trying to

sound confident. "In a doorway . . . near a warm chimney. I can sleep anywhere."

Billy sighed. "Come on. You can stay in the stable where I work. It's warm and dry there. Come morning, I'll send you to someone who can help."

Chapter 4

Safe

On the way to the stable, they passed the bridge again.

"Something special, aine it?" Billy said. "They're calling it the Eads Bridge, after the boss himself—James Buchanan Eads."

"Did you help build this bridge?" Everett asked.

"Yep," said Billy. "Mr. Eads figured out a way to piece it together, but it was us former slaves who did most of the work. A lot of folks said it couldn't be done. But see how wrong they were."

"Is it safe to walk across?" Everett asked.

The young man laughed. "Been up since eighteen seventy-four and it hasn't fallen down yet. Trains go across it every day."

Billy's place turned out to be just a one-room shack beside Brooks's Livery Stable. Even so, it was warm and comfortable inside.

That evening Billy fried up a skillet of potatoes and several slabs of smoked bacon while he told Everett about the livery. "Mr. Brooks is a blacksmith. He buys, sells, and boards horses. The U.S. Army hired him to break and train some of their horses. And Mr. Brooks hired me to get them saddle-ready. He's a fair and honest boss. That's enough for me."

While they ate, Everett told Billy how he had gotten to St. Louis.

"I want to get away West," he said.

"What are you running from?" Billy asked quietly.

"A farm that don't grow nothing but dirt. And my worrisome brother. Gus frets about everything." Everett blew out his breath and warmed his hands by the fireplace. "He clucks over me like a hen in britches."

"Ever thought that might be 'cause he cares about you?"

"What Gus cares about is the land . . . the land . . . the land. My other brother, Cole, is in the Tenth Cavalry out in Indian Territory," Everett said proudly. "I want to meet up with him someday. Hey," he said. "Cole might be riding a mount you trained, Billy."

"Now wouldn't that be something?"

After dinner was cleared, Billy took a lantern and said, "Come, let me show you where you'll bed down for the night."

There must have been two dozen stalls in the stable. "That's Hard Tack, Martha Gray, and Queenie," Billy said, pointing out one horse after another. At last he found an empty stall.

"Now we've got a full house," he said. "It aine a bit fancy, but the hay is warm and dry. Just be careful of Shadow."

As soon as he said that, the horse in the next stall kicked the gate so hard the whole stable shook.

"See what I mean?" said Billy. "I've been working with him for weeks. No luck."

From a safe distance Everett studied Shadow. The horse was beautiful—a big brown quarter horse with black stockings, black tail and hair. Everett reached out to rub the horse's nose.

"No!" shouted Billy. "Don't bother him."

Later, when Everett was alone in the stable,

Shadow kicked and stomped restlessly.

"Shhh, big fella," Everett told Shadow. "Everything's going to be just fine." Then Everett sang "Oh, Susannah," one of the songs from back home. Finally the horse settled down.

Everett snuggled under the two quilts Billy had given him. He rubbed the medal in his pocket. Good luck had come his way. He was warm. His belly was full. Best of all, he had found a friend.

Chapter 5

Help

"Will you write down where I have to go?" Everett asked the next morning.

Billy's face clouded over for a moment. "Look here," he said. With a stick, he made a few lines in the ground. It was a map. Billy showed Everett the path he had to take. "I'm sending you to Reverend Able Johnson. His church sits on the corner of Eleventh and Lucas. He helps all the Exodusters."

Everett put the directions in his head.

"Go straight there, you hear? Be careful. This

town is full of people who would do you harm. You saw that yourself yesterday."

Everett promised to be careful and went on his way.

A winter storm was coming, and the wind made it feel colder than it was. The sky was pale gray, and a light snow was falling. Everett passed a small market and a brewery. Soon a wagon rumbled by. He hopped on the back and rode to the center of town. There he found Lucas Street.

He was about to cross to the other side when a horse and buggy came roaring around the corner.

"Watch out!" a girl cried out.

Everett jumped back but fell.

"Are you a'right?" The girl was staring down at him now.

Everett wanted to answer, but he couldn't stop looking at the young woman. Her eyes were large and round. Her skin was smooth and the color of chocolate.

"Am I alive or dead?" Everett asked.

The girl laughed.

Everett stood and brushed dirty snow from his pants.

"Well, you look to be alive, so I'll be on my way." She started to leave.

"Oh, oh," Everett moaned, holding the side of his head. "I do believe I feel a little dizzy."

The girl gave him a look that showed she wasn't fooled. "Where are you going?"

"I'm looking for St. Paul Church—it's at Eleventh and Lucas," Everett answered, smiling broadly. Then he remembered to look pitiful. "I'm looking for Reverend Able Johnson."

"You are!" she said in surprise. "Well, follow me. I'm Hattie. And it so happens, Reverend Johnson is my father."

Chapter 6

—⚬—

Looking Forward

Several women were serving a noonday meal to about fifty people in the basement of the church.

When an elderly lady holding a cooking spoon saw Everett and the girl, she called over her shoulder, "Izetta, Hattie's brought one more for lunch."

Hattie went to the kitchen to help. Everett joined the group at a nearby table. They were Exodusters, just like Billy said. Folks from Mississippi. Folks from Louisiana. One family was from Tennessee, not far from Pearl.

"All we want is the chance to own a piece of land and the peace to farm it," said a man from Arkansas.

A family of eleven had walked to St. Louis all the way from Hopkinsville, Kentucky. Klansmen had burned their farm. "The Klan sure wants to keep us down. Every time any-body tries to pull theirselves up, stand like a man, here them night riders come to burn down our homes and fields. We lost everything—barn, furniture, livestock—everything," the father said.

"But we have each other," said his wife beside him. She took the man's hand. "And we have our health and strength. We will make a new start."

"I've been sharecropping since freedom come.

That's 'most fifteen years. Aine much better'n slavery. Out West maybe I'll get to work my own place," a Mississippi man told Everett.

Land. Everybody was talking about going out West to farm. *I could have stayed in Pearl, Tennessee, to do that,* Everett thought.

"And what about you, son?" one of the Exodusters asked Everett.

"When I'm eighteen, I want to join the cavalry like my brother. But right now? I don't rightly know," he answered honestly. "All I know is I don't want to be a farmer. I don't want to grow anything . . . not even flowers!"

All eyes turned toward Everett. He was sorry he'd opened his mouth.

"Well, listen to you. Aine you got big plans!" one woman said, laughing.

"What you gon' do, if not farm?" a woman asked.

"I can read and write. I'll find work," said Everett.

"See, Delila," said an elderly man sitting next to the woman. "He's free-born, got book learning, too, like our Jake. They don't think like us who was slaves. Their dreams are bigger."

"That's right. And it's good to look forward, but you should never burn the bridge that brought you over," said another Exoduster. "Reading and writing is fine. But farming is important, too. Land don't care if you got learning or not. Them that owns land got power. You can never own enough farmland."

Everett had heard Gus say those same words many times. "Our pa fought a terrible war," Gus always began the story. "He came home and bought this farm. Worked the rest of his life to make sure it was paid for. He left it to us free and clear."

Staying on the farm—that was Gus's dream. But Pa had sent Everett to school instead of to the fields. "You can lose the land to thieves, but they can never take your learning," he said. He wanted Everett's dreams to be bigger than his.

Chapter 7

❧

Whispering

When lunch was over, Hattie brought Everett to meet her father. "Daddy, this is Everett Turner," she said.

Everett shook hands with the Reverend Able Johnson. He was handsome in a princely way, with a slight build, dark skin, keen eyes, and a quick smile.

"You're mighty young to be heading West alone," Reverend Johnson told Everett. "Got any family?"

"My pa and ma are dead. I'm by myself, sir,"

was all Everett said. "Billy Breeze said you would help me."

"Ah," said Reverend Johnson. "He's one of the finest horse trainers in town. Some say he's a horse whisperer."

"A horse whisperer?"

"Folks say he can talk to horses," Hattie put in. "There's not a horse he can't handle."

"You haven't seen Shadow," Everett said, and told her about the quarter horse.

"Now, how can I help you, boy?" the Reverend asked.

"I want to go West, soon as I can," said Everett. "Near where the Tenth Cavalry is."

"Tenth Cavalry, you say? Why, I know all about those soldiers. First blacks to be soldiers in peace time."

"That's right," Everett said proudly.

Reverend Johnson put his hand on Everett's

shoulder. "That's Apache and Comanche Indian Territory," he said. "The government isn't letting settlers in there. But a group is leaving for Kansas come May, after the weather breaks. That's as far west as you can get now."

May! That was four months away. Kansas? That wasn't where Cole was.

"Can't I just go on my own? I'm not afraid."

Reverend Johnson raised an eyebrow. "You should be afraid," he said. "Out West is a mighty big place. It takes time to get ready for such a long trip. And getting there is hard. Settlers must learn to work together to survive. Wait till spring. The West isn't going anywhere."

Everett left the church, disappointed. It had stopped snowing, and the sun had come out. It reminded him of what his pa used to say: A winter sun is pretty but it won't keep you warm.

Everett made his way back to Brooks's

Livery. "I can't get close to where my brother is, but there's a group leaving for Kansas in May," he told Billy. "I need a job and a place to stay till then."

Billy got Mr. Brooks to hire Everett as a stable boy. "Ten cents a day and bed in the stable," said the big red-bearded man who was his new boss. A handshake sealed the deal. "You can start today."

Everett soon found out that taking care of horses was hard work. No glamour. Cleaning out stalls, shoveling hay, and grooming were part of his chores. It was worth it, though. All the farm back home had was one old mule. Everett had never been around horses before. And they took to him right away. Lucky liked to be stroked on his flank. Queenie loved apples. Hard Tack whinnied whenever Everett came to bed down for the night. But Shadow was his favorite. Shadow was proud, like a king.

Every night, Everett spoke to Shadow in the next stall and sang to him. His music seemed to soothe the horse.

Every morning Everett greeted Shadow, saying, "Hi, big fella." But Shadow always backed away, stomped, and snorted.

"Leave him be," Billy told Everett. "That horse has a lot of healing to do before anybody can work with him."

Billy was leading Martha Gray, a black, white, and gray mare, out to the corral as he spoke. Everett followed.

"What happened to Shadow?" Everett asked.

Billy answered, "Can't say for sure, but somebody hurt that horse something awful."

"How? Why?" Everett wanted to know.

Billy saddled up Martha Gray. He shrugged. "I don't know how or why. I just know Shadow is scared. And he needs to feel safe and cared for before he trusts a rider again. The army was going to put him down. But I bought him from them for next to nothing. And Mr. Brooks takes his board out of my pay. I don't know if it was a bargain or not. I haven't been able to reach him."

"Are you what they say—a horse whisperer?" Everett asked.

"Some people think I am. Animals, especially horses, tell me things."

"They talk to you?"

Billy shook his head. "No, not like you and me talk. But from the time I was a little boy, I *knew* what dogs and horses were feeling. Take Shadow for example. He's saying 'leave me alone.' So I'm honoring his wishes. Then again he may not choose to speak to me. Animals are like that, you know?"

"What do you mean?"

"We think we choose animals to belong to us. It's really the other way around. They choose us. They'll let you know if you listen."

"Can anyone be a horse whisperer?" Everett asked.

"My pa always said what I have is a gift. Can't be taught or bought."

Everett watched Billy put the bit in Martha Gray's mouth. She reared up. Billy took the bit out and rubbed her neck. "Shhhh, I didn't forget, lady," he whispered. Then he asked very politely, "May I ride you today, Miss Martha?" The horse immediately calmed down and let Billy mount her.

That night in the stable Everett dreamed that he and Cole were soldiers. They were charging into battle. Everett was in uniform. His horse was big and brown with black stockings. It was Shadow.

Chapter 8

———❦———

Found

On Sunday Everett almost skipped church to sleep late. But he'd that heard Pap Singleton was going to speak. He didn't want to miss that. Pap Singleton was the leader of the Exodusters.

The church was full. Everett's eyes searched the room for Hattie. He spied her up front, beside an older woman. Everett guessed that she might be Mrs. Johnson, Hattie's mother.

When Hattie saw Everett, she waved. She sure was something pretty to look at. Everett waved back just as morning worship started.

Afterward, people stayed to hear Benjamin "Pap" Singleton.

He wasn't a big man, but his presence filled the space. He had wavy, mixed gray hair, and his white beard gave him a distinguished appearance. But his callused and twisted hands showed that he was a man used to hard work. In a booming voice, Singleton began. "Brethren, friends, and citizens all, I greet you in the name of the Divine Creator. To those who don't know me, my name is Benjamin Singleton. Back in Tennessee where I'm from, people call me 'Pap'—short for 'Pappy.' I represent the Tennessee Real Estate and Homestead Association out of Nashville. And I've come to tell you about a wonderful place called Nicodemus, Kansas."

There were many amens, and someone shouted, "Tell us about Nicodemus."

Singleton didn't hesitate. "The town hasn't been settled more'n a year. Kansas is flat as a pancake, and you got to go far to find a tree. So the first families pitched tents and made dugouts. The Indians helped them. And they built houses out of sod. 'Soddies' they call them. Then an early snowstorm came, but those brave pioneers—men, women, and children—survived the long, hard winter. Now they are ready to build more permanent houses and plant crops. Soon it will be a place anybody would be proud to call home."

In his mind Everett could almost see the town the way Pap described it would be.

"There will be a school for your children to attend; fields to labor in; respect and equal rights under the law for everyone," Singleton said. "In Nicodemus, the winters are long and the summers are hot as blazes, but it doesn't matter that your skin is black. You and your families—you'll live without fear of the Klan. No more violence. Leave all that behind. Kansas offers us a new day, a new way."

Again there were shouts of amen. Singleton held up his hand. "All of you are welcome. But the group we're taking out in May will help get the town ready for more settlers. We have a teacher already. Miss Jenny Fletcher. But we need carpenters, blacksmiths, coopers, and wheelwrights. I'll be back Wednesday to sign up people who can help us build a town. Your town!"

People burst into applause. Everett was clapping the loudest. There must be a place for a person like him. A person who could read and write.

"Come see me about joining up on Wednesday. Right here!" Pap Singleton said, waving a white handkerchief over his head. "We're going away West! Away West!"

The crowd began to chant and wave white pocket-handkerchiefs, too. "Away West! Away West!"

Everett was caught up in the excitement. Then he felt a hand on his back and glanced over his shoulder.

His worst nightmare had come true. Gus was sitting behind him. His eyes were full of anger. Gus had found him!

"I aine going back," Everett said, a little too loudly. As the people in his row left, Everett tried to run. But Gus grabbed his arm.

"I aine going back!" Everett resisted.

"Lower your voice," said Gus. "You're in God's house. I've come to take you home. And that's that."

At that awkward moment, Hattie approached

them. "Hello, Everett," she said cheerfully.

Everett tried to conceal his anger. "How-do, Miss Hattie." He noticed she was staring at Gus and waiting. "And—uh—and this is my brother Gus," he said flatly.

"I knew you must be brothers," she said, grinning widely. "You both have the same cut of jaw, and those jug ears are a dead giveaway."

Gus tipped his hat and said, "How-do, ma'am."

"Are you heading West with Everett?"

"No, ma'am. I am not. I been worried sick since he run off. I'm here to take him home."

"Everett, you ran away?" Hattie asked.

"He didn't tell you that?" Gus was frowning.

"No, he did not." Hattie turned toward the door of the church. Reverend Johnson was standing there with Pap Singleton. "My father doesn't know it either."

Chapter 9

Face-to-Face

"Everett, you said your ma and pa were dead. You never said you had a brother home worrying about you." Reverend Johnson sounded disappointed. But he showed the brothers into his office where they could talk thing over in private.

Gus paced the floor. Everett stood at the window with his back turned.

Finally, Gus said, "It's a miracle I found you. But I took a chance that you'd follow Cole's footsteps. My prayers have been answered. For that I'm grateful."

Everett shrugged. "I've done fine on my own. Made friends. I have a job and a place to stay."

"That's all well and good. But we're still going home," Gus said, turning Everett around so they were facing each other. "What in the name of all that's holy do you expect to do out West? You have no money. No skills. No nothing."

Everett pulled away. "You can take me back. But I'll run away again and again and again," Everett said sharply. "Anyway, I got a lot of book learning. I'll find something."

Gus rubbed his forehead with the heel of his hand. "It's all that stuff Pa put in your head about being free. If book learning got you to thinking that freedom means doing whatever you want, then it's better to stay ignorant. You may be smart, but you don't know nothing 'bout life."

They were silent for a moment. Gus pulled an envelope from his pocket. "Got a letter here from Cole. You want to read it?"

Everett quickly unfolded the paper and read it.

Dear Brothers,

At this writing I am alive and well. Life is hard out here in New Mexico. The food is terrible. I'd give a year's wages for a hot bath and a good night's sleep in a real bed with clean sheets. The Apaches are not going to give up their land without a fight. Many lives will be lost.

Even though we are on opposite sides, the Indians admire our courage in battle, and our kinky hair reminds them of the buffalo. So they call us "Buffalo Soldiers."

The sad part is, out here there is enough land for everybody. No need to fight over it.

Your brother,
Cole Turner

Land again! thought Everett. *That's what Cole was in the army fighting Indians for?*

Gus allowed Everett to keep the letter. Everett took out Pa's medal and looked at it.

"I see you still have the medal," Gus said, touching it in his brother's hand.

"It means a lot to me," Everett said softly, folding the letter and placing it and the medal in his pocket. "Almost as much as going out West."

Gus looked away. There were creases of worry in his forehead. "Everett, I'm going to speak to you man to man." There was a different tone in Gus's voice now. "I promised Pa I'd hold on to our land. But the truth is, I can't much longer—not without help. I have to make a good crop this year or we'll lose everything. I won't force you to come back, but I am asking you."

Everett felt bad. Still his mind was made up. He wasn't going back with Gus. But he needed time to think how to say no in a way Gus would accept.

"Give me till Wednesday to decide," was all he said.

Chapter 10

The Lie

Gus agreed to wait until Wednesday for Everett's answer. Meanwhile he took up the Reverend's offer to stay in the parsonage attic.

On Monday it started snowing again, and for the next two days it didn't stop. St. Louis was under four feet of snow. By Wednesday the temperatures had fallen dangerously low. Still a large crowd gathered for the meeting at St. Paul.

When Everett arrived, he joined Gus, who was sitting next to Hattie.

Reverend Johnson called for Gus to give the opening prayer. Back home, Gus was often the leader. But this was a big city church and the room was full. Everett closed his eyes, hoping that his brother wouldn't sound like a country bumpkin.

Gus's prayer was sincere and moving. "Dear Father in Heaven, we ask that your holy spirit stop by this place. Spread the warmth of your loving mercy over those of us who have gathered here in your name. . . ."

His voice sounded so different—not like he sounded when he was calling hogs or shooing the chickens. There were plenty of amens shouted from the deacons' corner.

Hattie seemed impressed. Her face lit up when Gus came back to sit between them.

Then Pap Singleton spoke. "Whatever skills you have can be put to use in Nicodemus. So don't be shy. Come forward now."

Gus turned to Everett. "I know what your answer is. I can tell by the look on your face."

"Gus, I can't go back to Pearl. I can't. I got it all planned. First, Kansas. And when I'm old enough, I'll join the army and be with Cole." Then Everett hurried over to get in line.

"What can you do, young fella?" Pap asked Everett.

"I can read and write," Everett said proudly. "Yes, sir. I went to the eighth grade. My pa told me that with schooling, I could do anything."

"Your pa was right, son. But we have a teacher already. Can you lay bricks? Do carpentry? Shoe horses? If not, you can come on the next trip."

"No. Please. I want to go on this trip," Everett

said. Then words began popping out of his mouth. "I—I—I break horses. Billy Breeze and I are partners, good friends. We've been working together . . . awhile. . . . He's a horse whisperer, you know."

"Now that's more like it. I know who Billy Breeze is—everybody around here does," Singleton said. "You are lucky to have him as a friend and teacher."

Pap Singleton thought for a moment. "I think we can find use for a good horseman, especially one trained by Billy Breeze. Sign right here."

Everett did. But he felt no excitement. Instead he felt sick to his stomach.

Then Hattie came rushing up. She pulled him over to where Gus and Reverend Johnson were talking to several Exodusters.

"Everett signed up," Hattie announced cheerfully.

"I wish you well, little brother," Gus said. His eyes looked tired and sad. "Pa would be proud."

Everett wanted to fall in a hole.

"I'll be heading home then," Gus went on. "But I'll come to say good-bye."

"Oh, you won't be leaving us so soon. No boats can go anywhere, not with the river frozen like it is," said Reverend Johnson. "Until the river thaws, you're welcome to stay on. You can help out with the Exodusters. I sure could use a hand."

"Good idea. A great idea!" said Hattie, smiling broadly.

It surprised Everett when Gus quickly agreed.

"Why are you so quiet?" Hattie asked Everett.

Everett tried to say something, but he couldn't. Outside, Everett gulped in the icy air and ran back to the stable. Alone there, he buried his face in his hands. He had told a lie. A wicked lie. The medal felt heavy in his pocket. The captain of the *Camel's Back* was right. He didn't deserve it. And Gus was wrong. Pa would not be proud of him at all.

Chapter 11

---·⌘·---

Busted

The next day Everett watched Billy work for hours with the horses, even in the deep snow. Everett studied his every move.

"Never use a whip on horses," said Billy. "You can beat them into obeying you. But you'll never beat them into being loyal."

"Did you learn that working here?" Everett asked.

"No," Billy answered. "I learned that when I was a slave." Then under his breath he added, "That's about all I learned."

That night, Everett lay awake on his straw bed. Shadow was restless again. He kicked and bucked in his stall. Everett sang every song he knew, until at last, the horse quieted.

Then an idea began to form. His singing always calmed Shadow. Maybe Everett could ride Shadow by singing to him. *How hard could it be?* Everett whispered to himself in the darkness. *Climb on! Hold on! Sing!* Then what he had told Pap Singleton wouldn't be a lie.

The next morning, Everett woke before dawn. Billy wasn't up, yet. It was icy cold. Everett got the saddle ready. Slowly he led Shadow out of his stall. Outside, puffs of breath floated around their heads.

"It's okay, big fella," Everett said, throwing a rope around Shadow's neck. "It's me, your pal." The horse bucked and reared, pulled on the rope, and kicked at the frozen ground.

"Come on, Shadow. I'm not going to hurt you." Everett began singing, a soothing song. One that the horse liked.

Shadow stood as still as the best battle horse. He patiently allowed Everett to buckle the saddle on and put the bit in his mouth. Shadow followed Everett out of the stable and to the corral. He didn't move a muscle while Everett mounted him.

"Good boy," Everett said, patting Shadow's strong neck. He started singing, "Oh, Susannah, oh, don't you cry for me. . . ."

In a burst of energy, Shadow began bucking and kicking. Everett held on while the horse hurled him around like a sheet flapping in the wind. "No, Shadow!" Everett shouted, forgetting about singing. Then just as abruptly, Shadow stopped still, as if giving in to Everett. But Shadow had a mind of his own. Once again the

horse reared up, and this time Everett went flying.

As he hit the ground, sliding, his mouth filled with icy dirt. He spat it out, gagging. He rolled over, out of Shadow's way. His forehead throbbed. His hand touched a bloody gash over his brow. He tried to take a deep breath, but the world went dark.

When Everett came to, he was lying on Billy's bed. A doctor was bandaging his forehead.

"What . . . what happened?" Everett asked.

"A nasty cut. *And* you got the wind knocked out of you," said the doctor. "You're a lucky young man. Nothing seems broken. Your ribs got banged up a bit. And you'll have a scar to remember the ride."

"I told you Shadow wasn't ready!" Billy said, then stomped off.

There was nothing Everett could say, because Billy was right.

Everett closed his eyes and slept a little. The next time he opened them, he felt better. His head was clear. Gus was sitting beside the bed.

"Gus! I'm sorry," he said. "I really messed up."

Trying to sound cheerful, Gus said, "Hey, I'm here. I'll stay till you can take care of yourself."

It would have been better if Gus was mad. Everett turned away. He couldn't look at his brother.

Billy came with an armload of wood for the fireplace. He put on a log and poked the fire. "I've tried to watch out for Everett, but . . ."

Gus held up his hand. "Oh, I know how stubborn he is."

"He's got no patience."

"And no discipline," Gus added.

"He doesn't know how to listen," Billy followed.

"Stop talking like I'm not here!" Everett shouted. "I can hear everything."

"Yes, but are you listening?" asked Billy and Gus at the same time.

Chapter 12

———— ◈ ————

Teachin' and Learnin'

The next morning, Everett got up and dressed. He was very sore but his head had stopped pounding. "I hope you aine too angry with me," he said to Billy.

"Not as much as I should be!" Billy said, and smiled. But then Billy didn't know the whole truth. Everett was miserable. He touched the medal.

"Pa always told me I was smart," Everett blurted out. "He said all my schooling would get me to wherever I needed to go. I thought I could help teach in Nicodemus. But Pap Singleton says they've already got a teacher. He wasn't going to let me sign up."

Billy listened as Everett rushed on.

"That's when I told him I could break and train horses. I said *you* taught me. I told him we were partners. I *have* to go West, Billy. That's why I lied—that's why I tried to ride Shadow."

Billy sighed deeply. "You did a foolish thing by making me a part of your lie," he said. "Now you got to fix what you done."

Everett shrugged. "How? I'd give anything to be a good horseman," he said.

Billy turned away, mumbling, "I'd give anything to read and write."

"What? What'd you say?"

Billy turned. "My master wouldn't allow slaves to have no book learning. You'd get whipped if you were caught with a book. I want to know what the Good Book really says. Not what my master said it said."

Everett understood. He used to read the Bible to his pa. "That aine what they tol' us," Pa used to say when Everett read aloud Scripture.

"I can teach you to read and write," he told Billy.

"Really? I'd be mighty tickled just to write my name. I hate using an *X*."

Everett took the poker from the fireplace. In the ashes he made a *B*. "That's *B*. It's the first letter in both your names."

Billy took the poker. His hand was shaking. He made a *B*. His letter was wobbly. Still, it was a *B*. Billy smiled. "Look at that! I wrote a letter," he whispered, then he shouted it. "I wrote the letter *B*!" Everett had never seen Billy so happy.

One by one, Everett made all the letters—*A* to *Z*. Billy copied each one.

"We'll do more this evening," said Everett.

"Everett, you told Pap Singleton that I trained you. Well, I can change that lie to the truth. You teach me to read, I'll teach you about horses."

Then Billy put out his hand. Everett shook it and headed for the stable.

Everett was so excited he couldn't stop talking. "Can I start now? Right now? C'mon, Billy!"

Billy held up his hands. "Whoa! First lesson. Training horses takes patience," he said, laughing. "First, you must calm yourself. You're much too noisy inside and out to be a good trainer. Every good horseman starts by being a good listener."

"I've got ears. I'm listening," Everett mumbled under his breath.

"Ears don't make you a listener, no more'n eyes make me a reader. You must learn to hear—

really hear what a horse says to you."

Billy put the bit in Martha Gray's mouth. "May I ride you today, Miss Martha?" Everett remembered Billy had said that before.

The horse pawed at the ground with her front feet. She shook her head. Her tail flicked from side to side. Then she snorted. Billy smiled. "Did you hear her answer?"

"I think she said no," Everett replied.

"You weren't listening. She just told me I could ride her. She gave me her permission, because I had the courtesy to ask."

"What?" Everett laughed. "I didn't hear any of that."

"I know," said Billy, smiling.

Leaning against the fence post, Everett watched Billy with the horses. Everett was way too sore to ride. But he tried his best to listen.

Later that night when they had eaten, Billy

took the poker in hand. He made another *B*. "What comes next in Billy?"

Everett showed him. He wrote *B-I-L-L-Y*. He called out each one of the letters. Then he made its sound. "There it is—Billy. That is your first name."

Billy took the poker. He made a *B*. It still looked wobbly. His *I* was longer than the other letters. He forgot one of the *L*s. Billy threw the poker down. "I'm too old for this."

"You have to be patient," said Everett, calmly. "We're just beginning. You are way too noisy inside and out to be a good student. You must learn how to see the letters, hear their sounds. . . ."

Billy chuckled hearing his own words being thrown back at him. Then his face turned serious. "I understand, Everett. It's hard to be patient when you want something so much."

Chapter 13

Change of Heart

Two weeks passed. During the day, Everett was the student, working alongside Billy. He learned to hold the reins with confidence, and how to tuck and roll when he was bumped off.

At night, Billy was the student, learning the alphabet by memory. Soon he could write his full name. So Everett began teaching him to read simple words and the numbers from one to a hundred.

One evening Gus came to visit. He had

another letter from Cole. Everett was so excited, he read the letter out loud.

My dear brothers,

I am alive and well at this writing. I hope this letter finds you likewise. I think of you both so often.

We are family. With Ma and Pa gone, all we have is each other. I never knew that until I was away from you.

My work is long and hard. They use us to escort the mail, repair telegraph lines, and patrol the area, keeping out settlers and treasure hunters. In New Mexico, the days are blazing hot and the nights are cold. The mountains are beautiful, but scorpions and rattlesnakes rule the desert.

The Apache will not stay on the reservations that the government has set aside for them, so they run away. Our orders are to bring them back. I understand why they run. But I am a soldier. I must obey orders.

Before it is over a lot of people on both sides will die. Keep me in your prayers.

Your loving brother,

Cole

When Gus was ready to leave, Everett pulled him aside. "The river's starting to thaw, Gus. Don't you need to get back? Planting season will be coming soon."

Gus shrugged. "I'm not going right back. I'm thinking of wiring Lee Jenkins. Ask him to sharecrop our land this season. If he can't, I'll pay somebody else."

"Pay? Gus, we don't have any money," said Everett. "You aren't staying on account of me, are you?"

"Well, yes . . . no. Truth is, Reverend Johnson wants to hire me to help with the Exodusters. He asked me to teach Bible study on Wednesdays. And I'll lead prayer service. I want to stay," said Gus. "I want to go home, too. But something is keeping me here for a reason." He paused before speaking again. "I love talking the Good Book with the Reverend. I want to learn to be a preacher."

Everett looked at Gus straight in the eye. "Do what makes you happy." Then Everett shook his head playfully. "I think Miss Hattie is the reason you're staying! Are you going to marry her?"

Gus gasped. "Marry? I just met Hattie a few days ago!" he sputtered.

"Don't wait too long," said Everett. "You'll still be thinking about it, and she'll have gone and married somebody else."

That night, Everett lay awake listening to the

horses breathe. Gus had changed. Gus was trying to follow his dream.

Leading prayer service! Can you imagine that?

Shadow kicked 'the gate. "Good night, big fella," Everett called. "I'm not mad at you. It was my fault." Then he closed his eyes, as he fell asleep humming "Yankee Doodle."

Chapter 14

Failure

Spring came early, in March. The last of the snow melted. The winds brought Midwestern thunderstorms that awakened the seeds that burst into bloom. It was a glorious spring that lifted everybody's spirits. May was not so far away. Everett had used some of his wages to buy a bedroll, a frying pan, and other supplies for the trip. He also had his eye on a pocketknife he was saving up to buy.

Everett had learned so much from Billy. He had broken in a young horse named Ginger. But

Ginger wasn't like Shadow. She was like a puppy dog—she loved to please.

One morning after breakfast, Billy was leading Shadow out of the stable for exercise. Everett came up slowly. "Good morning, big fella," he said, reaching his hand out, palm down. Shadow came forward and put his head under Everett's hand. Shadow snorted.

"Well, sir," said Billy, looking surprised. "Aine you two the best of friends?"

"I've been working at it since the day I got here. But he's finally let me touch him. Or as you can see, he touches me."

Billy thought for a while. "Tell you what. He's yours today," Billy said.

"Do you think I'm ready?" Everett tried not to show too much excitement.

"We'll soon see."

Everett took two big breaths. To be tense might make Shadow nervous. But Everett's heart was pounding. Sweat formed on his brow.

Shadow stayed calm when he was in a stall and by himself with Everett. But this was different. Would he let him ride?

Everett quietly saddled Shadow. He climbed up. Instantly, Shadow reared back on his hind legs and kicked. Everett held on.

Then the horse bucked and kicked and bucked some more. Just when Everett thought there wasn't another kick left, Shadow bucked again. Everett went sprawling to the ground. But Billy had taught him how to fall. So this time he didn't get hurt.

Everett touched the medal in his pocket. "I'm not giving up," he whispered.

Billy watched from the fence rail. "You're too

tight," he called. "Loosen up! Loosen up!"

Everett was determined. He mounted Shadow. Once again, Shadow threw Everett off. On again. Off again. On again.

"You're trying too hard. That's the problem," Billy shouted from the fence rail. Everett wasn't fully mounted when Shadow flipped him off like a worrisome fly.

Billy stepped in. "Everett, that's enough for today. You have to know when to quit. Enough."

Everett felt like his legs could not hold him upright. He wanted to cry but willed the tears back. His eyes stung and his throat burned.

He was too sore to eat. Too hurt to talk. So he went to bed early. No lesson for Billy tonight. *Who am I trying to fool?* he thought. *I'll never be ready to join the group going to Kansas.*

That night Everett didn't sleep much.

Shadow was restless, too. In the morning, he hurried to find Gus. "Need to talk," he told him.

Gus found a private place in the church courtyard where they sat on a stone bench. "What's the matter, Ev? You look like a cat lost in high cotton."

Everett took the medal from his pocket. "Why didn't Pa give this to you or Cole? Why me? I don't deserve it."

Gus answered. "Pa had high hopes for you, because—"

"I know. I know!" Everett broke in. "Because I was born free."

"No, not just that. He knew he was going to die before you reached manhood. Me and Cole knew Pa; we had him around much longer. He gave you the medal so you would keep a memory of what he stood for—honesty and bravery."

"And I aine neither," Everett said. "I lied to Pap Singleton. . . . You're the one with the courage. You and Cole."

He told Gus the whole story. Gus patted him on the back and asked, "What will you do if you don't go West?"

"Go back home with you, I guess."

"Trouble is, Everett, I don't know if I'm going home. I feel like God is calling me to stay here. Preach. I didn't come here with the idea of staying. But how do I ignore God's call?"

Everett shook his head. "You can't."

"No more than you can ignore your call to go West. You've done a lot to get this far. Some of it wrong. But you're learning."

"Tell me what to do, Gus," Everett pleaded.

"I can't. I been doing that for too long. I can't keep crowding you. You've got spirit, little brother. And strength. You helped me see I have dreams of my own. And I thank you for that."

On the way back from the church, Everett walked along the waterfront, thinking and wondering. He stopped right in front of the *Camel's Back*. Maybe the captain still had a job for him. But then Everett thought, *No, that's running again*. So he turned back toward Brooks's Livery, instead.

Chapter 15

Success

When Everett got back to the stables, he looked for Billy. There was a message in the ashes: *Store*. So Everett knew Billy would return shortly.

Meanwhile, Everett went back to the stables and saddled Shadow and walked him to the corral.

"It's just you and me," Everett said. "So no reason to get jumpy." He stroked Shadow's neck. He was saying those words for the two of them. Then he mounted Shadow, and immediately the horse tried to buck him off. But Everett hung with him. Without Billy there, Everett felt calmer. If Shadow went left, Everett easily leaned into it just as Billy had taught him. Spinning. Turning. Rearing up. Everett moved his body with Shadow's, not against it.

At last Shadow stopped. Snorted. Shook his head and circled the corral in a nice slow canter.

On the other side of the corral, coming toward Everett, was Billy. When he saw Everett, he gave a whoop and a holler. "Are you a horseman or what?"

"I'm going to Kansas," the boy whispered, giving Shadow a squeeze.

Later on, while he was shoveling hay, he told Shadow, "No more giving up! Did you hear that?"

Everett sang while he worked. He changed the words to fit his happy mood:

I got shoes.
You got shoes.
All of God's children got shoes.
When I get to Kansas
Gon' put on my shoes
And gonna strut all over God's Kansas!

The horse seemed to loved it. So he sang it
again—louder.

Chapter 16

Heading Out

From that day forward, Everett and Shadow were always together. Shadow loved to rest his nose on Everett's shoulder and blow out a breath of air. "He wants me to sing, when he does that," Everett said, smiling.

Most nights when Hattie and Gus stopped by the livery, Gus brought the newspaper. Now that it was late April, it stayed light out much later. Billy could read bits from the newspaper now. Everett followed any news of Cole's regiment.

Everett came to see he would be lucky to

make it to Nicodemus. Going out to where Cole was would be impossible.

Some nights Billy read from the Bible. Billy could find any scripture by book, chapter, and verse. Even though he still couldn't read all the words.

"You'll get better as you practice more," said Everett.

"Won't be the same without you giving me a hard time about being patient and all," Billy answered.

No it wouldn't be the same without Billy and Shadow, Hattie and Gus and Reverend Johnson, and all his friends, thought Everett. But the departure date for Kansas had been set for May tenth. And he was ready.

The day came quicker than he imagined. Everett woke to a cloudless sky.

"What a beautiful day to start a new life,"

said Hattie. She and Gus had come to the river-front to say good-bye.

All the time Everett was talking to them, he was wondering when Billy would show up.

"There'll be a church in Pearl, at last," Gus told Everett. "The church will lease land from us to build a small church and a school. I'll need you and Cole to approve the lease."

"You know we will," said Everett.

"When I am ordained, I will be preaching there." Then Gus looked over at Hattie and added, "And with the help of the Lord, my future wife will teach in the school we start."

"You'll make it happen," said Everett. "I know you will, especially with Miss Hattie here by your side." Hattie's eyes suddenly filled with tears. She hugged Everett and wished him well on his journey.

The brothers were silent for a moment. There

were a thousand things Everett wanted to say. "Gus," he said at last. "I want you to know that I'll miss you."

Gus grabbed Everett and hugged him close. "I will miss you, too, little brother. Take care of yourself, and may God watch over you every step of the way." With a good strong squeeze and a pat on the back, Gus stepped back and let Everett stand on his own.

"Until we meet again," said Gus.

"Until then," said Everett.

Just then, Everett saw Billy coming down the wharf, walking Shadow behind him. Everett shouted to him, "I thought I was going to leave without getting to say good-bye."

"I'm here, aine I?" Billy grinned. Then he placed Shadow's reins in Everett's hands.

Everett was too stunned to speak.

"Every horseman should have a good mount," Billy said. "Besides, this horse chose you. He never talked to me the way he does you. I may own him, but he is not mine. He is yours, and if you left without him, he would miss you something awful."

Everett heard what Billy was saying. "Billy, I will miss you, too," he said.

Just then Pap Singleton came over. "Billy Breeze," he said, extending his hand. "They say you're one of the best horsemen around. I'd love to have you come along with us. We could sure use a man like you."

"I can truthfully say, you already have a good horseman," said Billy. "Everett Turner. I trained him, so I know."

Everett stood by listening to Billy tell how good he was with horses.

"He told me you were his teacher," said Singleton. "That's what made me sign him up. I had my doubts—him being so young and all."

"Everything I said, I'd sign my name to it," said Billy. And he looked at Everett and winked.

Then, with the wave of his hat, Pap Singleton called out to the Exodusters, "Are we ready?"

"Yes!" folks shouted in a thunderous voice. They began boarding the boat that would take them up the Missouri River to Kansas City. From there, they would form a wagon train that would go to Nicodemus.

Everett joined the line. He patted Shadow's neck. "It's you and me now, big fella," he said. Then Everett turned once more to wave to Gus, Hattie, and his good friend, Billy. How long would it be till he saw them again?

Everett touched the medal in his pocket. For

the first time, he felt like it was really his. "Pa, I'm following my dream," he whispered.

Then with a nod of his head, Pap Singleton shouted, "We're heading away West!"

Another Scrap of Time

"**E**verett Turner was my grandfather," said Gee. She pulled a photograph from the trunk. It was of a young boy sitting on a beautiful horse.

"This is Everett and Shadow. See it says, '*Summer 1880. Nicodemus, Kansas.*' "

They all looked at the picture. Then they put it in the scrapbook.

"Let's make a shadow box for the medal," said Trey, holding up the Civil War medal. "I know how. We did one at school. Then we can hang it up."

Gee agreed that they would do that the next time they were together.

"Did Great-Great-Grandpa Everett become a Buffalo soldier, same as his brother Cole?" Mattie Rae asked.

"Everett enlisted in the Tenth Cavalry in eighteen eighty–four at the age of eighteen," said Gee. "He worked with the horses. He served until eighteen eighty–eight. Here is a copy of his discharge papers. He was part of the company that captured the Apache warrior Geronimo." Gee helped them put Everett's discharge papers in the scrapbook.

"What did he do after that?" Aggie asked.

"He settled in Kansas City, Missouri. He was a grown man the next time he saw his brothers. Everett got married and had four sons and two daughters—his younger daughter was my mother."

"We remember her from the story you told us about when you were a girl and the lunch counter sit-ins," Aggie put in.

"What happened to Gus? Did he marry Hattie? Did they have children?" Trey asked.

Gee laughed. "Hold on, let me try to remember all your questions. Gus became a preacher in Pearl, Tennessee. And yes, he did marry Hattie, and they had five children."

"And what about Cole?" Aggie wanted to know.

"Cole came back to Pearl, too, after the army. He never left home again. He and his wife raised five children on the family farm. And to this day, members of the Turner family still live there and attend St. John Church, built on land that once belonged to Franklin Turner."

"We had the family reunion in St. Louis one year," Aggie said. "That was before you were born," she told Mattie Rae.

"It isn't the fourth largest city in the country anymore. But it is still called the Gateway to the West. Thousands of people came through St. Louis, going West, every year. They crossed the Eads Bridge, which is still standing." Gee showed the children a postcard of the bridge. They put it in the scrapbook.

"What about Billy?" said Trey. "What happened to Billy?"

"I don't know," said Gee. "I've often wondered about him. One thing, he is not forgotten. Whenever the Turners get together, we tell stories. And Billy Breeze is very much a part of our family's history."

"What is this?" said Aggie. She held up a magazine called *The Crisis*.

"Oh, my goodness. I've been looking for that! Inside there's a poem written by one of my aunts," said Gee.

"Read it to us," pleaded Mattie Rae.

"Next time," Gee said, putting away the scrapbook. "Next time."

Timeline

∙❦∙

Remembering the Past

I live in St. Louis in the shadow of the Eads Bridge mentioned in this story. The city's Gateway Arch honors everyone who passed through the city on their way West. So it was fascinating for me to learn more about the pioneers who were African-Americans. Here are some of the important events that spurred former slaves and their families to leave the South.

Patricia C. McKissack

✦ 1840: The St. Paul African Methodist Church is established in St. Louis, the first African-American church west of the Mississippi River.

✦ 1865: After the Civil War ends, Jefferson Barracks near St. Louis remains a military base where civilian blacks find work such as breaking horses for the cavalry.

✦ 1866: Congress authorizes the all-black ninth and tenth cavalry regiments and four infantry units. The black soldiers are nicknamed "Buffalo Soldiers" by the Native Americans they encounter.

✦ 1867: The first national meeting of the Ku Klux Klan is held at the Maxwell House Hotel in Nashville, Tennessee. The group has been terrorizing newly freed blacks by burning their homes, schools, and businesses. Because of the Klan, many black families decide to leave the South in search of a better, safer life.

✦ **1874:** The Eads Bridge, a double-tiered bridge that former slaves helped build, opens in St. Louis.

✦ **1877:** Former slave Benjamin "Pap" Singleton (1809–1892) begins leading groups of fellow freedmen to create all-black settlements out West. He helps more than twenty thousand people start new lives.

✦ **1877:** A group of pioneers arrives in Nicodemus, Kansas. In the town's heyday in the 1880s, six hundred people live there. Other famous all-black towns develop at the same time.

✦ **1879:** The church-led Colored Refugee Relief

Board helps hundreds of black Southerners (called "Exodusters") heading out West. Many arrive in St. Louis with no money and no place to stay. Later the Colored Immigration Aid Society also helps pioneers on their journey.

✦ **1976:** Nicodemus, Kansas, is declared a National Historic Landmark. Today only twenty-two people still live in the town.